To Amira ~ A B

For my sweet Helena
and her friends ~ K N

LITTLE TIGER PRESS LTD,
an imprint of the Little Tiger Group
1 Coda Studios,
189 Munster Road,
London SW6 6AW
www.littletiger.co.uk

First published in Great Britain 2019

Text copyright © Anna Bowles 2019
Illustrations copyright © Kasia Nowowiejska 2019
Anna Bowles and Kasia Nowowiejska have asserted their rights to be identified as the
author and illustrator of this work under the Copyright, Designs and Patents Act, 1988
A CIP catalogue record for this book is available from the British Library
All rights reserved
ISBN 978-1-78881-061-6 • LTP/1400/2384/1018
Printed in China
2 4 6 8 10 9 7 5 3 1

FAIRYTALE CLASSICS

Little Mermaid

Anna Bowles

Kasia Nowowiejska

Little Tiger
LONDON

At the bottom of the sea lay the kingdom of the merpeople.
Crabs scuttled over the rocks, fish went swish through the
weeds and oysters played catch with pearls.

Six beautiful mermaid sisters
lived together in a coral
palace. They hung bells
from their tails and wove
shells into their hair.

But the youngest little mermaid was not
interested in shells and bells. She sat around
getting bored, bored, BORED!

"I wonder what's on the surface?" she thought. The youngest mermaid swam up to find out.

The sky was wide and bright, and seagulls called.
Right in front of the little mermaid was . . . a ship!

On board the ship, humans
were laughing and dancing.

They looked so happy!

A storm was coming, but nobody on the ship seemed to notice. The little mermaid shouted and waved.

As the thunder rumbled and the rain beat down, the ship rocked, and the prince tumbled into the sea!

The little mermaid dived under the waves to rescue him.

The little mermaid used all her strength
to drag the prince to the shore.
"Can you help Prince Nathan?"
she begged a passing girl.

The girl looked unsure. "He's so messy," she said.
But the little mermaid glared hard at her, and
the girl decided not to argue.

When the little mermaid got home, she couldn't
stop thinking about Prince Nathan.
So she went to see the sea witch in her cave.
  "I want to have legs so I can
walk on land and dance
with the prince."

"Hmm. Legs?" croaked the witch.

"Yes!" said the little mermaid.

"To walk?"

"Yes!"

"And dance?"

"Yes!"

"OK. If you insist," said the witch.

"Here's the deal. I'll make you a potion if . . .

. . . you give me your voice so I can be a
Singing Superstar!"

The little mermaid agreed, and
the sea witch cast a spell to take
the mermaid's voice.

"La-la-la ... la-la-la-la
la-la-la-la-la
la-la-la-laaaaa!"

"Excellent!" cooed the witch, delighted with her new voice.
But the little mermaid had no voice to reply. She would be
silent forever! She took the bottle and swam up to the surface.

When the little mermaid swallowed the witch's
magic potion, she felt very strange.
    She let out a BUUUURP!
    Her stomach rumbled, BLOIK!
    And her tail transformed into two beautiful legs!

She was able to stand up,
just like a human.

Of course, walking
takes some practice.

And dancing
takes even more.

As she was practising, Prince Nathan came riding by!

The silent mermaid shivered and nodded hard. The prince wrapped her in his cloak and took her back to the castle.

"Princes always marry princesses," explained Prince Nathan to the little mermaid. "It's just how things are."

When the prince met the princess, things got even worse for the little mermaid.

You're the girl who looked after me when I was shipwrecked! How could I not marry you?

The little mermaid sat on a rock and cried. She was heartbroken. If she'd had a voice, she might have said something rather rude.

The prince tried to comfort the little mermaid,
but he didn't know what was wrong.

Suddenly the princess said, "I know you! You're the mermaid who saved Nathan from the storm."

"You used to be a mermaid?!" exclaimed the prince. The little mermaid nodded.

You saved my life. You're amazing!

At last the prince realised that he was in love
with the little mermaid, and with her help
he found the courage to tell his father.

They were married that day. And when
the mermaid opened her wedding
present from the sea witch,
a magical thing happened.
Her voice came back!

Everyone sang and danced until dawn.
But the most sweet-voiced, graceful and
happy of all was the little mermaid.